Flower Fairy Tales
of the
Language of Flowers

Volume I

The Flower Fairy

HOW

THE POET JACOBUS

SUPPOSED HE HAD FOUND A SUBJECT FOR AN

EPIC POEM.

THE CHAPTER CONTAINS A SUMMARY OF EVERY
THING WHICH THE ANCIENTS AND MODERNS
HAVE WRITTEN ON THE LANGUAGE OF FLOWERS.

Alphabetical List of Flower Meanings

---

by Taxile Delord, translated by N. Cleveland,
edited by m stewart, illustrated by J.J. Grandville

earthly pursuits (www.earthlypursuits.com)
2010

FOREWORD

Flower Fairy Tales of the Language of Flowers are taken from *The Flowers Personified*, a strange and delightful book. The original work is *Les Fleurs Animees*, illustrated by J.J. Grandville and written in French with an introduction by Alphonse Karr, text by Taxile Delord. First published in Paris in 1847, it was translated by N. Cleveland and published in the U.S. also in 1847 as *The Flowers Personified,* with hand-colored steel engraved illustrations by J.N. Gimbrede from designs by J.J. Grandville.

J.J. Grandville is the pseudonym of Jean Ignace Isidore Gérard (1803-1847), a French artist famous for caricatures and fantastical illustrations. In addition to political cartoons, he illustrated editions of *Gulliver's Travels*, the fables of Jean de La Fontaine, *Robinson Crusoe, Don Quixote* and other books. *The Fleurs Animees* illustrations were a lithographic collection.

Taxile Delord (1815-1877), a French author and editor.

Alphonse Karr (1808-1890), a French critic, journalist and novelist. ("Plus ça change, plus c'est la même chose." The more things change, the more they stay the same.)

Nehemiah Cleaveland (1796-1877), an American writer, historian and translator.

J. N. Gimbrede (1820-?), an American engraver.

Flower Fairy Tales of the Language of Flowers tells the stories of the flowers' lives after The Flower Fairy allowed them to go live as humans in the world. The Flower Fairy was displeased that the flowers wanted to leave her to become human. Their tales, for the most part, are not happy.

Volume I includes: "The Flower Fairy"—a tale about why the flowers wanted to become human; "How The Poet Jacobus Supposed He Had Found A Subject For An Epic Poem: A Summary Of Everything Which The Ancients And Moderns Have Written on the Language of Flowers", including an alphebetical list of flower names in English, French and Latin with their meaning; and a bonus alphabetical listing of flower meanings.

The Language of Flowers is an ancient language, eloquent, exclusive and just as subject to misinterpretation and error as any other language. Different cultures have used it throughout history. Flowers, herbs, shrubs and trees were assigned meanings that people familiar with The Language of Flowers could "read" by knowing the sentiment symbolized by the plant. The combination of flowers in a bouquet and the way they were worn or given to each other held meaning. Hours of the day ("Flora's Clock"), days of the week ("The Floral Week") and the months of the year ("The Calendar of Flora") were also assigned a flower meaning. Coded messages could be exchanged and secret meetings arranged, if you knew the language.

There are many Language of Flowers "dictionaries" and they do not all agree on what each flower means.

The alphabetical lists of flower names and flower meanings are a popular resource for names for babies, pets, characters and web IDs.

Enjoy!

m stewart, editor

The Flower Fairy.

Learned antiquaries have ascertained and plainly described the spot where the earthly paradise was situated. We know with what trees those celestial grounds were planted, and what countries adjoined them on the north, the south, the east, and the west. Thanks to these researches, the topography of Eden would appear to advantage in the charts of the Land Registry, or among the files of the Recorder of Deeds.

No philosopher has busied himself in determining exactly the geographical site of the palace occupied by the Flower Fairy. We are left, in this respect, to mere conjecture. Some place it in the kingdom of Cashmere; others say it is on the table-land of the Himalaya, others suppose it to be situated in the center of the island of Java; in the midst of some vast forest, which, by its labyrinthine and prolific vegetation, protects it from unseasonable visits, and from the research of exploring travelers.

We alone are acquainted with the route to the Flower Land—but a solemn oath forbids us to reveal it. The newspapers would get there as soon as we could and God only knows to what condition they would soon bring that happy country, which as yet, has experienced no revolution, but the one which we are about to describe.

If the reader would accompany us thither, he must suffer his eyes to be bandaged. We must also examine his pockets, lest, like Tom Thumb, he scatter seeds on the way, to identify his path.—Now we have commenced our journey, and the bandage may drop as soon as we arrive.

Do you not feel around your brows a softer and sweeter air than you ever breathed before? Do you not perceive, in spite of the obscurity that veils your sight, a light more brilliant, and penetrating, and delightful, even than that which shines on your native land? It is because our journey is accomplished. We are now in the domains of the Flower Fairy.

Here is a garden where the productions of every zone and clime are united, and live together in friendly brotherhood. The brilliant tropical flower is seen by the side of the violet, and the aloes near the periwinkle. Palm-trees spread their fan-like leaves above a grove of acacias, whose white flowers are faintly tinged with red. Jasmines and pomegranates mingle their silver stars and their crimson glow. The rose, the pink, the lily, and a thousand flowers which arrest the eye, but which we need not name, here mingle in harmonious groups, or form beautiful arabesques. All these flowers live, breathe, and converse, as they interchange odors.

Round the feet of the trees, shrubs, and plants, countless little rills flow, wildly meandering. The water runs over diamonds, whose light flickers and plays, as it comes reflected with tints of gold, of azure, or of opal. Here butterflies of every shape and hue, shun or chase each other in their mingled flight. Now they float—now wheel—now alight— and now rise, with wings of amethyst, of emerald, of onyx, of turquoise, and of sapphire. There is not a bird in the garden,—yet you seem to be enveloped by a universal harmony, as in one of the concerts which we hear in our dreams—and this is the breeze which sighs, murmurs, plays, and sings some melody to every flower.

The palace of the fairy is not unworthy of this wondrous place. A genius, who is her friend, has collected those threads of silver and gold, which in the mornings of early spring, float from plant to plant. These he has braided, interwoven, and formed into graceful festoons. The whole palace is composed of this charming filigree. Rose-leaves form the roof, while the blue bindweed fills the interstices of the light trellis which extends like a curtain round the fairy—who, indeed, is seldom at home, occupied, as she is, in visiting her flowers, and watching their happiness.

Does any one think that a flower can never be unhappy? It would seem to be impossible—and yet nothing is more certain. Our fairy found this by her own experience.

One fine spring evening, as the Flower Fairy was gently rocking in her hammock of interwoven convolvuli, idly thinking of those other mysterious flowers, which we call stars, suddenly she thought she heard a distant rustling—a confused noise. "It is the sylphs," thought she, "who come to woo the flowers;" and she relapsed into her revery. But soon the sounds became louder, and the golden sand resounded under steps more and more distinct. The fairy sat erect, and beheld approaching a long procession of flowers. They were of all ages, and of every rank. Full-blown Roses, already on their decline, there walked, surrounded by their young families of buds. All distinctions were overlooked. The aristocratic Tulip gave her arm to the vulgar and plebeian Pink. The Geranium, proud as a financier, walked side by side with the tender Anemone—and the haughty Amaryllis listened without much disdain, to the rather vulgar conversation of the Bladder-nut-tree. As often happens in well arranged societies, at times of great emergency, a forced reconciliation had taken place among the flowers.

Lilies, with their brows encircled by fireflies and Bellflowers, with glow-worms shining, like living lanterns, among their petals, lighted the procession, which was brought up, in a somewhat disorderly manner, by a careless troop of Daisies.

The procession drew up in good order before the palace of the astonished fairy, and an eloquent Hellebore, stepping from the ranks, thus addressed her:—

"Your Majesty:

"The flowers here present beg you to accept their homage, and to lend a favorable ear to their humble complaint. For thousands of years we have supplied mankind with their themes of comparison; we alone have given them all their metaphors; indeed, without us poetry could not exist. Men lend to us their virtues and their vices; their good and their bad qualities;—and it is time that we should have some experience of what these are. We are tired of the flower-life. We wish for permission to assume the human form, and to judge, for ourselves, whether that which they say above, of our character, is agreeable to truth."

A murmur of approbation followed this speech.

The fairy could not believe the testimony of her own eyes and ears.

"What," said she, "do you wish to change your existence, so like to that of the gods, for the miserable life which men lead? What is there wanting to make you happy? Have you not, for your adornment, diamonds of dew?—conversations with the zephyrs for your entertainment?—and the kisses of butterflies, to make you dream of love?"

"The dews make me take cold," said, with a yawn, the Belle de Nuit.

"The songs of the Zephyr tire me to death," said a Rose. "He has repeated the same thing for these thousand years. The poets of an academy must surely be more amusing."

"What care I," murmured a sentimental Periwinkle, "for the caresses of the Butterfly, since he never participates in the enjoyment? The Butterfly is the very symbol of selfishness. He would not know his own mother,—and his children, in their turn, would not recognize him. How can he have learned any thing of love? He has neither a past, nor a future; he remembers nothing, and is himself forgotten. Men alone know how to love."

The fairy turned upon the Periwinkle a mournful look, which seemed to say,—"And *thou*, too!" She felt that her efforts to put down the rebellion would be unavailing,—still she resolved to make one more attempt.

"Once upon the earth," said she to her revolted subjects, "how do you intend to live?"

"I shall be an author," replied the Wild-rose.

"And I a shepherdess," added the Corn-poppy.

"I shall come out as a marriage-maker,—I as a schoolmaster,—I as a teacher of the piano,—I as a trinket-vender,—and I as a fortune-teller"— exclaimed all together, the Orange-flower, the Thistle, the Hortensia, the Iris, and the Daisy.

The Larkspur talked of his debut at the opera, and the Rose vowed that when she should have become a duchess, she would have the satisfaction of crowning *rosières** without number.

Many flowers were there which had already lived, and which declared that life among men was very comfortable and agreeable. Narcissus and Adonis had been the secret instigators of this revolt,—especially Narcissus, who longed to know how a beautiful youth would look in a Venetian mirror.

The Flower Fairy remained for a while plunged in thought. She then addressed the rebels in a sad but decided voice:—

"Go, deluded flowers;—let it be as you propose. Ascend upon the earth, and try human life. Ere long you will come back to me."

The history of these flowers, which were changed to women, you will read in this volume. We have collected these adventures wherever we could find them,—traversing all lands, and questioning all classes of people,—but keeping no record of dates or epochs. The flowers have lived, to a certain extent, everywhere. You may have been acquainted with some of them, and not suspected it. It is very unfortunate that they have not thought fit to make more disclosures, or to write their own memoirs. This would have relieved us from much trouble—would have saved us many steps, and more than all, many mistakes.

---

*Young maidens who have won the prize of goodness.

In concluding this introduction, we must inform you that the fairy did not grant the desired permission, without silently resolving that she would be revenged. The next morning her garden was a desert. One flower alone remained—the solitary Heath-plant, which blooms perpetually.

Symbol of undying love ! she well knew that for her there was no place on earth.

HOW

THE POET JACOBUS

SUPPOSED HE HAD FOUND
A SUBJECT FOR AN

EPIC POEM.

THE CHAPTER CONTAINS A SUMMARY OF EVERY
THING WHICH THE ANCIENTS AND MODERNS HAVE
WRITTEN ON THE LANGUAGE OF FLOWRS.

————————————

Heartsease

Pensée   *Viola Tricolor*

I.

THE FLOWERS CONVERSE.

The Pansy* was wandering about the earth, not knowing where to find a home.

She had knocked at door after door, and found no admittance. Then she offered herself as lady's companion to a celebrated blue-stocking, and was refused.

A philosopher of high renown declined receiving the Pansy, even as a housekeeper.

Repulsed successively by an academician, a minister of state, a preacher, a painter, a novelist, and a sculptor, poor Pansy determined to leave the town, and resume her wanderings.

It was a fine spring morning when she set out on her journey. She had not much to carry—but she was firm, resigned, and prepared to endure bravely the inconveniences of her lot.

Plunged in meditation, the Pansy walked on, unconscious of the length of the way. Evening at length overtook her; she began to feel weary, and casting her eyes around, she looked for some place where she could seek refuge.

She saw, at a short distance from the road, the front of a château brightly lighted up, and towards it she turned her steps. The owner, seated at his table, which was spread under a tent of silk upon the terrace, was singing, drinking, eating, and laughing with his friends.

"Admit me," said a feeble voice, which reached, nevertheless, the ears of the guests.

---

*La Pensée,—Thought.
"And there is pansies, that's for thoughts." [Ophelia, in *Hamlet*.]

"Who are you?" said the host. "If you are a merry companion, and know how to lighten the heavy hours, come in."

The voice replied, "I am the Pansy."

"Servants, shut the gates. Drive away this dull intruder—this troublesome companion, who causes us to remember. Let us forget! Let us forget!"

The master of the château filled his cup, and drank to Forgetfulness.

"I noticed, yonder, a modest cottage," said the Pansy, who, to rest herself, had leaned for a moment upon a marble vase, that stood near the entrance of the château. "The poor are always hospitable: I will seek there a shelter for the night. I am fatigued, and begin to feel the cravings of hunger."

She took the path to the cottage.

Knock!—knock!—knock!

"Who is there?"

"A night's lodging, if you please."

"If you can content yourself with a morsel of bread, a glass of water, and a little fresh straw, come in:—but first tell me who you are."

"I am the Pansy."

"Accursed one, avaunt! You come to disturb my slumbers. I have to-day been watering with my sweat my master's fields. Now he is indulging in the pleasures of the festive board, while my wife is weeping, and my children have not bread to eat. If, to-morrow, I would have strength to resume my toils, it is necessary that I should forget. You disquiet both mind and body. Begone! I shall not open the door."

So, neither the rich nor the poor would have any thing to do with the Pansy. She sat down on the edge of a ditch, and supported her head with her hands.

A young man happened to pass that way. As he walked, he gazed at the stars, and uttered, in a low tone, words and phrases which made him open his mouth wide and stare wildly.

A stifled sigh from the Pansy apprized him that some sufferer was in need of his aid. He went up to the traveler, took her by the hand, and, seeing that she was handsome, though serious and thoughtful, he asked her, with a slight lisp, why she wept.

The Pansy replied, that she had traveled a long distance,—that she had in vain sought the hospitality of the cottage and the castle,—but that no one had been willing to receive her.

"Poor child!" said the young man, making at the same time a sort of tragic gesture.

He put his arm about the waist of the Pansy, and assisted her to rise. He then directed her attention to a faint light, which shone through a distant clump of trees.

"That is the small house in which I live. Come— you will there pass the night in safety. By what name shall I introduce you to my mother?"

"They call me," said she, hesitatingly, "the Pansy."

At that the youth clapped his hands in gladness, and went forward to show Pansy the way to the house.

The Pansy, in her turn, wished to know the name of her host. "I am a man of fancy," he replied, "known in the country as Jacobus the Poet."

He lived in a small house in the midst of the woods, with no one but his mother, who entertained him with fairy-tales and witch-stories. These narratives still delighted him, for he was scarcely eighteen years old. He had rosy cheeks and fair hair, and his large blue eyes seemed starting from his head. In the country he was considered handsome.

When the mother of Jacobus learned the name of her guest, she proceeded herself to set the table for Pansy. It will be strange, indeed, thought she, if this does not give my son the idea of some capital great book, that shall bring us money, and give him access to the prince. But the Pansy objected to having much done for her. A slight matter served for her refreshment. She soon recovered her vigor, and found herself in a condition to notice the scene about her.

The room in which they were, resembled a greenhouse, so full was it of flowers and shrubs. Some of these climbed up the walls—others hung in arabesque from the ceiling. Buds scarcely opened, were seen side by side with full-blown flowers. The petals of others, already faded, were gradually dropping off, but did not, for this, seem less beautiful. Books, open or shut, marked in some places by green leaves, to keep the favorite passages, were scattered here and there among the vases. The shelves in the library of Jacobus were either the branches of shrubs, or tufts of flowers.

With his eye fixed on the Pansy, the poet forgot to eat. Never had he seen a woman so handsome, or beauty so attractive. He was especially pleased with her calm, deep eye, which had only, it seemed, to rest upon any object in order to give it forthwith a delightful charm, and a sort of genial glow.

The Pansy felt it her duty to thank her entertainer, but at the first word of acknowledgment, Jacobus checked her.

"The house which thou enterest is blessed," said he, taking care to give each phrase its proper stop, and its due measure; "thy presence alone confers on man every good. Thou impartest vigor to the soul of the young; thou canst make young the heart of the old. In thy company the hours flow on, without our feeling weariness or satiety. Without thee, the days seem tedious, and Time, having wings no longer, crushes us under his feet. Stay in my house; whatever it contains is thine. Remain with me, fair traveller. Where canst thou do better?"

Jacobus did not add, that his mother's notion was also sprouting in his brain, and that he hoped to derive profit as well as fame from the sojourn of the Pansy.

She smiled at the simplicity of the youthful poet, but this did not prevent her from fully appreciating the kind reception he had given her. She determined to show herself grateful.

All that night, Jacobus was unable to close his eyes. The thought of having received the Pansy under his roof, threw him into a kind of fever. His heart beat quick—his temples were hot—and an unnatural lustre shone in his eyes. Finding that he wooed sleep in vain, he rose and went down to his library, thinking that the sight of his flowers would calm his spirit.

He entered and went up to a Hawthorn. As he bent over to inhale its perfume, he thought he heard a gentle voice, which proceeded from the depths of the white corolla.

"Draw in my breath, friend. A single one of my branches, hidden in the midst of the hedge, is sufficient to scent the whole neighborhood. I am the flower of early spring,—I am Hope."

"Jacobus! Jacobus!" said a clear voice.

The young man turned, and saw a Bindweed, which was looking at him with its little blue eyes, and which said,—"I yield myself to every passing breeze; I run this way and that, as may happen—hanging from the branches of the oak—winding among the heather—living sometimes with the great, and sometimes with the little. Do not forget me. I am Caprice."

"I represent the ties of love," exclaimed a Honeysuckle.

A Clematis then attempted to speak, but was interrupted by a Maple.

"I am the Maple, with brilliant flowers and strong limbs. I am the symbol of Reserve. Listen to my advice, Jacobus. Trust not the Clematis, which climbs slyly up the walls, and shows her little head at the edge of the window, where young maidens go at evening to talk. The artful Clematis gets possession of their secrets, and then goes and makes sport of them, with her comrades, the giddy Almond and the perfidious Ebony."

The Clematis was about to reply, but the Fern prevented her, and took sides with the Maple. The sincerity of the Fern is so notorious, that the Clematis did not venture to engage with such an adversary. She held her peace.

Jacobus could not get over his surprise. The flowers were alive; they talked to him; he could not hear too much from them.

"Think of me," said the Lilac. "I bear green leaves, and bunches of fragrant flowers. My countenance has an air of simplicity, and at the same time of coquettishness. I bloom early, and fade soon. I am the *first love!*"

"While the snow yet glistens on the gnarled branches of the oak, and on the turf of the meadows, a fringe of flowers appears on the border of its white mantle. Is it spring already? Or is it winter still? It is the time when the Primrose shows its saffron-tinted tufts. Come, gather the flower of *early youth.*"

With the first notes of the nightingale, I shed upon the air the perfume of my ivory flowers. I am the Lily of the Valley, Brother to the Lily, I love, like her, the banks of the stream, the deep shade of woods, the solitudes of the valley. When men see me, they think of springs that have passed away, and of former happiness,—and I comfort them by the assurance that this happiness will return."

"Bees come and buzz in my blossoms, and young couples love to walk beneath my fragrant shade. From my dried leaves men obtain a wholesome drink. My qualities are mildness, goodness, and utility. I am the Linden—the flower of *conjugal affection*."

"Everywhere my white stars are seen to sparkle in the midst of my branches. I allow my supple and flexible limbs to be trained as men please. They stretch me on palisades,—they twine me around arbors,—they spread me out like a curtain along the terrace of the castle, or make me wind round the windows of the cottage. I comply with every demand—I am happy in every situation. I am the jessamine—the flowers of Amiability—the friend of the butterflies and the bees."

Every flower, in its turn, spoke some word in the ear of Jacobus.

"I shall be," he said, "a great fool, forsooth, if I do not commit to paper what I have just heard. With the aid of all these charming things, I will write a short epic poem of sixteen cantos, which will secure to me the place of minister, or at least, of first valet de chambre to the king."

Jacobus did as he proposed. He passed a large part of the night in listening to the flowers. As they all spake in a learned style,—that is, somewhat diffusely,—he adopted the plan of abridging their discourse. Being quite methodical in his habits, he reduced to alphabetical order the following notes, which were to aid him in composing his little poem of sixteen cantos.

*As many of these English names are but little used, the French and Latin synonyms are given in parallel columns.

A.*

English	French	Latin	Meaning
Acacia,	Acacia,	Acacia,	Platonic love.
Acacia, rose,	Acacia, rose,	Acacia, rosea,	Elegance.
Acanthus,	Acanthe,	Acanthus,	Arts.
Almond-tree,	Amandier,	Amygdalus,	Thoughtlessness.
Aloes, parrot-bill,	Aloès, bee de perroquet,		Small talk.
Aloes, socotrine,	Aloès, socotrine,	Aloe, succotrina,	Bitterness and pain.
Amaranth,	Amaranthe,	Amaranthus,	Immortality.
American Aloe,	Agavé,	Agave Americana,	Security.
Angelica,	Angelique,	Angelica,	Inspiration.
Anthericum,	Phalangère,	Phalangium,	Antidote.
Arum,	Gouet, commun,	Arum vulgare,	Ardor.
Arum, fly-catching,	Arum, gobe-mouche,	Arum crinitum,	Snare.
Ash,	Frêne èlevè,	Fraxinus excelsior,	Greatness.
Ash-leaved, Trumpet-flower	Jasmin de Virginie,	Bignonia radicans,	Separation.
Aspen,	Peuplier tremble,	Populus tremula,	Groan.
Aster, china,	Marguerite-reine,	Aster chinensis,	Variety.

B.

English	French	Latin	Meaning
Balm,	Melisse citronelle,	Melissa officinalis,	Joke.
Balsam of Peru,	Baume du Perou,	Myroxylon,	Cure.
Barberry,	Epine-vinette,	Berberis,	Sourness.
Basil,	Basilic,	Ocimum,	Hatred.
Beech-tree,	Hêtre commun,	Fagus sylvatica,	Prosperity.
Bellflower,	Campanule,	Campanula,	Indiscretion.
Bellflower, pyramidal,	Pyramidale bleue,	Campanula pyramidalis,	Constancy.
Bindweed, purple,	Liseron pourpre,	Convolvulus purpureus,	Eminence.
Bindweed, field,	Liseron des champs,	Convolvulus arvensis,	Humility.
Bird cherry-tree,	Lauier-amandier,	Prunus padus,	Perfidy.
Black thorn,	Epine noire,	Prunus sylvestris,	Difficulty.
Bladder-senna,	Baguenaudier,	Colutea arborescens,	Frivolous amusement.
Bluebottle,	Bluet,	Centaurea cyanus,	Delicacy.
Borage,	Bourrache,	Borago,	Bluntness.
Box,	Buis,	Buxus,	Stoicism.
Bramble,	Ronce,	Rubus,	Envy.
Broom-rape,	Orobanche majeure,	Orobanche major,	Union.
Broom, Spanish,	Genêt d'Espagne,	Genista juncea,	Cleanliness.
Broom, prickly,	Genêt épineux,	Genista spiniflora,	Misanthropy.
Bryony,	Tame commun,	Tamus communis,	Support.
Buck-bean,	Menyanthe,	Menyanthes,	Quiet; repose.
Bugloss,	Buglosse,	Anchusa,	Falsehood.
Burdock,	Bardane,	Arctium Lappa,	Importunity.

Cactus,	Cactus,	Maternal love.
Catch-fly, night-flowering,	Siléné, fleur de nuit,	Silene nocturna,	Night.
Celsia, great flowered,	Celsie à Crete,	Celsia cretica,	Immortality.
Chaste-tree,	Gattilier commun,	Vitex,	Coldness.
Cherry-tree,	Cerisier,	Cerasus,	Education.
Chestnut-tree,	Chataignier,	Castanea,	Justice.
Chestnut-tree, horse,	Marronnier d'Inde,	Æsculus hippocastanum,	Luxury.
Christmas aconite,	Hellebore de Noël,	Helleborus,	Wit.
Cinquefoil,	Quinte-feuille,	Potentilla,	Beloved daughter.
Clove-tree,	Giroflier,	Caryophyllus aromaticus,	Dignity.
Columbine,	Ancolie,	Aquilegia,	Folly.
Coltsfoot, sweet-scented,	Tussilage odorant,	Tussilago fragrans,	Justice.
Coriander,	Coriandre,	Coriandrum,	Hidden worth.
Cornel-tree,	Cornouiller,	Cornus,	Duration.
Crown-imperial,	Couronne impériale,	Fritillaria imperialis,	Power.
Crowfoot, marsh,	Renoncule scélérate,	Ranunculus sceleratus,	Ingratitude.
Crowfoot, meadow,	Renoncule, bouton d'or,	Ranunculus acris,	Perfidy.
Currant,	Groseiller,	Ribes rubrum,	Thankfulness.
Cypress,	Cyprès,	Cupressus,	Mourning.

D.

Daffodil, common,	Narcisse des près,	Narcissus sylvestris,	Deceitful hopes.
Dahlia,	Dahlia,	Dahlia,	Novelty.
Dandelion,	Pissenlit,	Leontodon,	Oracle.
Daisy, double,	Paquerette double,	Bellis hortensis,	Affection.
Daisy, single,	Paquerette simple,	Bellis simplex,	Innocence.
Daisy, wild,	Marguerite des près,	Bellis perennis,	Dost thou love me?
Date-plum,	Plaqueminier,	Diospyros,	Resistance.
Day-lily, yellow,	Belle de jour,	Hemerocallis flava,	Coquetry.
Dittany of Crete,	Dictame de Crete,	Origanum dictamnus,	Birth.
Dittany, white,	Fraxinelle,	Dictamnus,	Fire.
Dock,	Patience,	Rumex,	Patience.
Dodder,	Cuscute,	Cuscuta,	Baseness.
Dragon-plant,	Arum serpentaire,	Arum dracunculus,	Dread.

E.

Elastic Momordica,	Momordique élastique,	Momordica elaterium,	Critique; hoax.
Enchanter's Nightshade,	Circée,	Cichorium intybus,	Frugality.
Everlasting,	Gnaphale,	Gnaphalium,	Perpetual remembrance.

F.

Fennel,	Fenouil,	Anethum fœniculum,	Strength.
Fern,	Fougère,	Filix,	Sincerity.
Fieldrush,	Jonc des champs,	Juncus campestris,	Docility.
Fig Marigold,	Ficoïde glaciale,	Mesembryanthemum chrystallinum,	Coldness of heart.
Fir,	Sapin,	Abies,	Height.
Flax,	Lin,	Linum usitatissimum,	Benefactor.
Foxglove,	Digitale,	Digitalis,	Occupation.
Funitory,	Fumeterre commune,	Fumaria,	Gall.

G.

Geranium, clouded,	Géranium triste,	Geranium nubilum,	Melancholy.
Geranium, rose,	Géranium rose,	Geranium roseum,	Preference.
Geranium, scarlet,	Géranium écarlate,	Geranium coccineum,	Stupidity.
Gilliflower, Mahon,	Giroflée de Mahon,	Cheiranthus mahoneus,	Promptness.
Gilliflower, stock,	Giroflée des jardins,	Cheiranthus incanus,	Enduring beauty.
Goats-rue,	Galéga,	Galega,	Reason.
Goosefoot,	Anserine ambroisée,	Chenopodium,	Insult.
Grape-vine,	Vigne,	Vitis,	Intoxication.
Grass,	Gazon,	Gramen,	Utility.
Grass, quaking,	Brise tremblante,	Briza media,	Frivolity.

H.

Hair-moss,	Polytric á urne,	Polytrichum,	Secret.
Hawthorn,	Aubépine,	Cratægus oxyacantha,	Hope.
Hazel,	Noisettier,	Corylus,	Reconciliation.
Heath,	Bruyére commune,	Erica vulgaris,	Solitude.
Helenium, smooth,	Hélénie d'automne,	Helenium autumnale,	Tears.
Hepatica,	Anemone hépatique,	Anemone hepatica,	Trust.
Hogbean,	Jusquiame,	Hyoscyamus,	Defect.
Hollowroot,	Adoxa,	Adoxa moschatellina,	Weakness.
Holly,	Houx,	Ilex,	Forecast.
Hollyhock,	Rose trémière,	Alcea rosea,	Fruitfulness.
Honesty,	Lunaire,	Lunaria,	Forgetfulness.
Honeysuckle,	Chévre-feuille,	Lanicera caprifolium,	Bonds of love.
Hop,	Houblon,	Humulus lupulus,	Injustice.
Hornbeam,	Charme,	Carpinus,	Ornament.
Hortensia,	Hortensia,	Hortensia opuloïdes,	Carelessness.
Hyacinth, expanded,	Hyacinthe étalée,	Hyacinthus elatus,	Benevolence.
Hyacinth, garden,	Hyacinthe d'Orient,	Hyacinthus orientalis,	The language of flowers.
Hyacinth, wild,	Hyacinthe sauvage,	Hyacinthus sylvestris,	Play.
Hybrid crinum,	Crinole hybride,	Crinum,	Delicate weakness.

I.

English	French	Latin	Meaning
Immortal flowers,	Immortelle,	Xeranthemum annuum,	Unfading remembrance.
Indian cane,	Balisier,	Arundo bambos,	Rendezvous.
Ipomea, scarlet,	Ipomée écarlate,	Ipomæa coccinea,	Embrace.
Iris,	Iris,	Iris,	Message.
Iris, flaming,	Iris flambe,	Iris flammea,	Flame.
Ivy,	Lierre,	Hedera helix,	Friendship.

J.

English	French	Latin	Meaning
Jamaica Plum,	Myrobalan,	Spondias myrobalanus,	Privation.
Japan rose,	Camellia,	Camellia japonica,	Gratitude.
Jessamine, common white,	Jasmin commun,	Jasminus officinale,	Amiability.
Jessamine, Spanish,	Jasmin d'Espagne,	Jasminum grandiflorum,	Sensuality.
Jonquille,	Jonquille,	Narcissus jonquilla,	Desire.
Juniper	Genévrier,	Juniperus,	Succor.

K.

English	French	Latin	Meaning
King's-spear	Asphodèle jaune,	Asphodelus,	Regret.

L.

Laburnum,	Cytise faux ébénier,	Cytisus laburnum,	Blackness.
Ladies' Bedstraw,	Grateron,	Galium,	Rudeness.
Ladies' Ear-drop,	Fuchsia,	Fuchsia,	Frailty.
Larch,	Mélèze,	Pinus Larix,	Audacity.
Larkspur,	Pied d'alouette,	Delphinium,	Levity.
Lavender,	Lavande aspic,	Lavandula spica,	Distrust.
Laurel,	Laurier franc,	Laurus,	Glory.
Laurestine,	Lauier-tin,	Viburnum tinus,	Delicate attentions.
Lichen,	Hépatique,	Lichen hepatica,	Confidence.
Lilac,	Lilas commun,	Lilac vulgaris,	Earliest love.
Lilac, white,	Lilas blanc,	Lilac alba,	Youth.
Lily,	Lis,	Lilium,	Majesty.
Lily, daffodil,	Amaryllis jaune,	Amaryllis lutea,	Pride.
Lily of the Valley,	Muguet de Mai,	Convallaria maialis,	Return of happiness.
Lime-tree,	Tilleul,	Tilia,	Conjugal affection.
Lucerne,	Luzerne,	Medicago,	Life.

M.

Madder,	Garance,	Rubia,	Calumny.
Madder, yellow,	Alysse saxatile,	Alyssum saxatile,	Tranquility.
Maidenhair,	Capillaire,	Adiantum,	Discretion.
Manchineel,	Mancenillier,	Hippomanes mancinella,	Betrayal.
Mandrake,	Mandragore,	Atropa mandragora,	Scarcity.
Maple,	Erable champêtre,	Acer,	Reserve.
Marigold, cape,	Souci pluvial,	Calendula pluvialis,	Presage.
Marigold, garden,	Souci commun,	Calendula officinalis,	Trouble.
Marshmallow,	Guimauve,	Althæa,	Beneficence.
Marvel of Peru,	Belle de nuit,	Mirabilis,	Timidity.
Meadow-saffron,	Colchique,	Colchicum,	Autumn.
Meadow-sweet,	Spirée ulmaire,	Spiræa ulmaria,	Uselessness.
Mezereon,	Lauréole bois gentil,	Daphne mezereum,	Desire to please.
Milfoil,	Achillée,	Achillea,	War.
Milkwort,	Polygala,	Polygala,	Hermitage.
Mistletoe,	Gui,	Viscum album,	Parasite.
Motherwort,	Clandestine,	Lathræa clandestina,	Concealed love.
Mugwort,	Armoise,	Artemisia,	Happiness.
Mulberry, black,	Muier noir,	Morus niger,	Devotedness.
Mulberry, white,	Murier blanc,	Morus albus,	Prudence.
Myrtle,	Myrte,	Myrtus,	Love.

N.

Narcissus, white,	Narcisse des poétes,	Narcissus poeticus,	Selfishness.
Nettle,	Ortie,	Urtica,	Cruelty.
Nightshade,	Morelle,	Solanum,	Truth.
Nosegay,	Bouquet,	Florum fasciculus,	Gallantry.

O.

Oak,	Chêne,	Quercus,	Hospitality.
Olive,	Olivier,	Oliva,	Peace.
Ophrys, fly,	Ophrise-mouche,	Ophrys myoides,	Mistake.
Ophrys, spider,	Ophrise-arraignée,	Ophrys arachnites,	Dexterity.
Orange-blossom,	Fleur d'oranger,	Flos aurantii,	Chasity.
Orange-tree,	Oranger,	Aurantium,	Generosity.
Osmunda,	Osmonde,	Osmunda,	Revery.

P.

Pansy,	Pensée,	Viola tricolor,	Thought.
Parsley,	Persil,	Apium,	Feast.
Pasque-flower,	Coquelourde,	Anemone pulsatilla,	Without pretension.
Passion-flower,	Grenadille bleue,	Passiflora cerulea,	Belief.

D. cont'd

English	French	Latin	Meaning
Peony, common,	Pivoine officinale,	Pæonia officinalis,	Shame.
Peppermint,	Menthe poivrée,	Mentha piperita,	Warmth of feeling.
Periwinkle,	Pervenche,	Vinca,	Sweet remembrance.
Persian Candy-tuft,	Ibéride de Perse,	Iberis semperflorens,	Indifference.
Pheasant's-eye,	Adonide,	Adonis,	Painful remembrance.
Pimpernel, red,	Mouron rouge,	Anagallis phoenicea,	Appointment.
Pine,	Pin,	Pinus,	Boldness.
Pineapple,	Ananas,	Bromelia ananas,	Perfection.
Pink, clove,	Œillet des fleuristes,	Dianthus caryophyllus,	True love.
Pink, musk,	Œillet mignardise,	Dianthus moschatus,	Childishness.
Pink, yellowish,	Œillet jaune,	Dianthus luteus,	Unreasonableness.
Plane-tree,	Platane,	Platanus,	Genius.
Polemonium,	Polémoine bleue,	Polemonium ceruleum,	Rupture.
Pomegranate,	Grenadier,	Punica granatum,	Foppery.
Poplar, black,	Peuplier noir,	Populus niger,	Courage.
Poplar, white,	Peuplier blanc,	Populus alba,	Time.
Poppy, corn,	Pavot coquelicot,	Papaver rhæas,	Ephemeral charms.
Poppy, white,	Pavot blanc,	Papaver albus,	Dormant affection.
Prickly-pear,	Raquette-figuier d'Inde,	Cactus opuntia,	I burn.
Primrose,	Primevère,	Primula,	Early youth.
Privet,	Troëne,	Ligustrum,	Prohibition.
Prune-tree,	Prunier,	Prunus,	Promise.
Prune, wild,	Prunier sauvage,	Prunus sylvestris,	Independence.

R.

Reed,	Arundo,	Imprudence; music.
Rest-harrow,	Ononis,	Obstacle.
Rose,	Rosa,	Beauty.
Rosebay, Willow-herb,	Laurier-rose, Nerium oleander,	Distrust.
Rosebud,	Epilobium spicatum,	Production.
Rose capucine,	Rosæ calyx,	Young girl.
Rose, hundred-leaved,		Splendor.
Rosemary,	Rosa centifolia,	Graces.
Rose, moss,	Rosmarinus,	Healing balm.
Rose, musk,	Rosa muscosa,	Voluptuous love.
Rose, perpetual,	Rosa moschata,	Capricious beauty.
Rose, Provence,	Rosa perpetua,	Unfading beauty.
Rose, single,	Rosa provincialis,	*Gentillessee.*
Rose, striped,	Rosa berberifolia,	Simplicity.
Rose, white,	Rosa variegata,	Warmth of heart.
Rose, wild,	Rosa alba,	Silence.
Rose, yellow,	Rosa canina,	Poetry.
Round-leaved Sundew,	Rosa lutea,	Infidelity.
Rue,	Drosera rotundifolia,	Surprise.
	Ruta graveolens,	Manners.

Reed, Roseau, Imprudence; music.
Rest-harrow, Bugrane arrête-bœuf, Obstacle.
Rose, Rose, Beauty.
Rosebay, Laurier-rose, Distrust.
Rosebay, Willow-herb, Epilobe à épi, Production.
Rosebud, Bouton de rose, Young girl.
Rose capucine, Rose capucine, Splendor.
Rose, hundred-leaved, Rose cent-feuille, Graces.
Rosemary, Romarin, Healing balm.
Rose, moss, Rose mosseuse, Voluptuous love.
Rose, musk, Rose musquée, Capricious beauty.
Rose, perpetual, Rose des quatre saisons, Unfading beauty.
Rose, Provence, Rose pompon, *Gentillessee.*
Rose, single, Rose simple, Simplicity.
Rose, striped, Rose panachée, Warmth of heart.
Rose, white, Rose blanche, Silence.
Rose, wild, Eglantine, Poetry.
Rose, yellow, Rose jaune, Infidelity.
Round-leaved Sundew, Rossolis à feuilles rondes, Surprise.
Rue, Rue Sauvage, Manners.

S.

Saffron,	Crocus,	Abuse.
Sage,	Salvia,	Esteem.
Sea-lavender,	Statice limonium,	Sympathy.
Sensitive plant,	Mimosa sensitiva,	Bashfulness.
Sensitive Hedysarum,	Hedysarum gyranus,	Agitation.
Silver-weed,	Potentilla anserina,	Simplicity.
Snowball,	Viburnum opulus,	Ennui.
Snowdrop,	Galanthus nivalis,	Consolation.
Southernwood,	Artemisia abrotanum,	Pain.
Speedwell,	Veronica amœna,	Fidelity.
Spindle-tree,	Evonymus vulgaris,	Likeness.
Star of Bethlehem,	Ornithogalum,	Idleness.
Star of Bethlehem, pyramidal,	Ornithogalum pyramidale,	Purity.
Starwort,	Aster,	Afterthought.
Strawberry,	Fragaria,	Goodness.
Strawberry of the Indies,	Fragaria indica,	Deceitful appearances.
Succory,	Cichorium intybus,	Frugality.
Sunflower,	Helianthus,	False riches.
Sweet Sultan, yellow,	Centaurea moschata,	Felicity.
Sweet William,	Dianthus barbatus,	Scorn.
Syringa,	Philadelphus,	Fraternal regard.

Safran,	Safran
Sauge,	
Staticé maritim,	
Sensitive,	
Sainfoin oscillant,	
Argentine,	
Boule de neige,	
Galanth perce-neige,	
Citronelle,	
Véronique élégante,	
Fusain,	
Ornithogale,	
Ornithogale pyramidale,	
Astère,	
Fraise,	
Fraise de l'Inde,	
Chicorée-amére,	
Soleil, [Tournesol]*	
Centaurée-amberboi,	
Œillet de poéte,	
Syringa,	

*The correct name is Tournesol. Soleil means sun. [Ed.]

T.

Tares,	Ivraie,	Vicia,	Vice.
Teasel,	Cardére,	Dipsacus fullonum,	Benefit.
Thistle,	Chardon,	Carduus,	Harshness.
Thornapple,	Datura,	Datura stramonium,	Deceitful charms.
Thornapple, purple,	Stramoine fastueuse,	Datura fastuosa,	Suspicion.
Thyme,	Thym,	Thymus,	Activity.
Tiger-flower,	Tigridie,	Tigridia,	Cruelty.
Toad-flax,	Muflier,	Antirrhinum,	Presumption.
Touch-me-not,	Balsamine,	Impatiens,	Impatience.
Tree Primrose,	Onagre,	Œnothera,	Inconstancy.
Tuberose,	Tubéreuse,	Polyanthes,	Voluptuousness.
Tulip,	Tulipe,	Tulipia,	Declaration of love.
Tulip, virgin,	Tulipe vierge,		Literary debut.
Turnsol,	Héliotrope,	Heliotropium,	The intoxication of love.

D.

Valerian, red,	Valériane rouge,	Valerian rubra,	Facility.
Violet Ivy,	Cobée grimpante,	Coboea scandens,	Knots.
Venus's Looking-glass,	Miroir de Venus,	Campanula speculum,	Flattery.
Vervain,	Verveine,	Verbena,	Sorcery.
Viburnum, prickly,	Camara piquant,	Lantana aculeata,	Severity.
Violet, sweet,	Violette odorante,	Viola odorata,	Modesty.
Violet, white,	Violette blanche,	Viola alba,	Candor.
Virginian Cowslip,	Gyroselle,	Dodocatheon meadia,	Divinity.
Virginian Spiderwort,	Ephémérine de Virginie,	Tradescantia Virginica,	Transient felicity.
Virgin's-bower,	Clématite,	Clematis,	Artifice.

W. Y. Z.

English	French	Latin	Meaning
Wake-robin,	Arum commun,	Arum commune,	Ardor.
Wall-flower,	Giroflée jaune,	Cheiranthus cheiri,	Faithful in misfortune.
Water-lily, peltated,	Nélumbo,	Nymphæa nelumbo,	Wisdom.
Water-lily, white,	Nénuphar blanc,	Nymphæa alba,	Eloquence.
Water-lily, yellow,	Nymphea jaune,	Nymphæa lutea,	Growing indifference.
Weeping-willow,	Saule pleureur,	Salix babylonica,	Sadness.
Wheat,	Blé,	Triticum,	Riches.
Whortleberry,	Airelle myrtille,	Vaccinium,	Treachery.
Wild Rose-tree,	Eglantier,		A poetical person.
Wild-service,	Alisier,	Cratægus torminalis,	Harmony.
Willow-herb, purple,	Salicaire,	Lythrum salicaria,	Pretension.
Windflower,	Anémone,	Anemone,	Abandonment.
Woad,	Réséda,	Reseda,	Modest merit.
Wood Anemone,	Anémone des près,	Anemone nemorosa,	Sickness.
Wood-sorrel,	Oxalide-alléluia,	Oxalis acetocella,	Joy.
Wormwood,	Absinthe,	Absinthium,	Absence.
Wreath of Roses,	Couronne de roses,	Corona rosarum,	Reward of virtue.
Yew,	If,	Taxus,	Sadness.
Zephyranth,	Zéphyranthe,	Zephyranthes,	Fond Caresses.

Jacobus passed the rest of the night in his armchair. He dreamed of being crowned in the capitol; that he was arrayed, as he marched, in flowing robes, and held in his hand a lyre of gold.

The first person he saw, on awaking, was the Pansy, who greeted him with a smile. He told her what had happened to him,—and wished to know whether he had been imposed upon by a dream, or whether flowers could really talk.

"It is I," said the Pansy, "who speak in them. Henceforth you will surpass every rival. The secrets which I have communicated, and which you were the first to know, will be a fruitful source of poetic inspiraton."

Jacobus kissed Pansy's hand, and asked leave to read the notes which he had written during the night.

But he had hardly finished the reading, when, crushing the manuscript in his hand, he threw it at Pansy's head.

"Wretched creature!" said he, "is it thus that you requite my hospitality? What would you have me do with this miserable stuff? It is, indeed, a flower-language which you have communicated to me; but it was invented more than a thousand years ago, in Persia, by an academician of Bagdad. Little children would laugh in my face, if I should repeat to them such nonsense. Know that we have altered this entirely. The flowers have now a different signification; and, to begin with yourself, let me tell you, that you are nothing but an old *intrigante*. Your name comes from *paonsée*,* solely on account of the resemblance which exists between your shape and colors, and those of the peacock.

---

*Paonsée,—Untranslatable; derived from paon, a *peacock*.

The literati discovered your true origin a long time ago. They are now employed in deciding to what flower belongs the right of representing that phenomenon of mind which we call *thought*. For the personification of that other intellectual faculty, which is called *memory*, we have the myosotis—a flower which all persons of intelligence call vergiss-mein-nicht."*

The mother of Jacobus, attracted by the loud talking, and discovering what was the matter, prudently set aside the eggs, coffee, and cream, which she had prepared for the traveller's breakfast. "My honey," cried she, "you are trying to humbug us with your flower-language. You must take us for Picards or Percherons, when you come here with such stories. I perceive that you are merely an intriguer, whom we must drive away. But first, to show you that you cannot impose upon us so easily as you imagined, I shall tell you a short story. You are now, my son, to learn how it happened, that your father had the end of his nose frostbitten."

After having coughed and spit, the mother of Jacobus commenced the following narrative:—

---

*Forget-me-not.

II.

WHERE WE SHOW THAT THE LANGUAGE OF FLOWRS MAY CAUSE A MAN TO LOSE THE TIP OF HIS NOSE.

"I loved Jacobus, and Jacobus loved me. We were both young, handsome, sensible—and we had made a mutual engagement to live for each other. But unfortunately, the will of our relatives kept us apart. To correspond was our only consolation."

Madame Jacobus here heaved a sigh—and then resumed her narrative.

"'Dearest,'" said Jacobus one day to me, 'we are beset with snares. How do we know that they will not, at some time, discover the hollow in the beech-tree, where we deposite our love-letters? That no unsafe person may get at our secret, I have brought you this little book, which will make you acquainted with a new language, unknown to the vulgar. Learn to read it, and above all, to write it accurately.'

"I took the book. Its title was—'The Language of Flowers: in a course of twelve lessons.'

"With what earnestness did I devote myself to this study! To confess the truth, the language of flowers does not, at first, seem very difficult. The verb has but three persons—the first, the second, and the third,—I, thou, he.

"It is thus conjugated:—

"*I love*. We present the flower horizontally, with the right hand.

"*Thou lovest*. The same flower in the same hand, but inclined a little to the left.

"*He loves*. The same flower is offered with the left hand.

"Two flowers denote the plural. A flower inverted means denial. Thus a yellow asphodel, with its head downwards and its stem up, signifies—'I do not regret you.'

"There are three tenses,—the present, the past, and the future.

"We express the present, by handing the flower on a level with the heart; we denote the past, when we present it with the hand inclined downwards,— and the future, with the hand raised as high as the eyes.

"If a substantive be used in place of the verb, we conjugate the flower with an auxiliary. Thus, the jessamine is the symbol of amiability. Presented upright, and in the right hand, it means—'I think you amiable.' Presented to the left, in the same hand, it means—'You think me amiable.' How fully, Jacobus, was your father a jessamine to me!

"Love had very soon engraved these principles upon my memory. In summer, a nosegay in my bosom revealed to him every thought. In the winter, when we have flowers no longer, their names, written on paper, made known to us the state of our affairs. About this time, Jacobus was preparing to set out for Paris, that he might see an uncle on whom our union depended. I still remember the note which he wrote to me at that time:—

"'Wormwood can do nothing against the real acacia. You know that I have a dragon of whortleberry. Away with the hollow-root! Lion anemone, thy acacia is in the American aloe. Banish the king's spear, and think of the mugwort of our next interview.

"'The myrtle as high as the heart, and the myrtle as high as the eyes, forever.

"'JACOBUS.'

"It was unnecessary for me to look into the dictionary, in order to translate this billet at once.

"'Absence has no power over genuine love. You know that I hate treachery. But away with all weakness! Rest assured that your love is in safe keeping. Banish all regret, and think of our happiness when we shall again see one another.

"'I love you, and shall love you always.

"'JACOBUS.'

"This letter fell into the hands of my guardian. But it was all Greek to him.

"I blessed the language of flowers, and I continued to study it with still greater ardor, when it came near depriving me of a husband, and you, Jacobus, of a father."

Here Jacobus thought it his duty to wipe off a tear.

"Some flowers open their petals at a particular hour of the day, and close them at some other hour which is known. Linnæus made a list of these. It is by this list that we reckon the hours in flower-language.

FLORA's CLOCK.

MIDNIGHT	....	The large-flowered Cactus.
ONE O'CLOCK	....	Alpine Sow-thistle.
TWO	"	Yellow Goats-beard.
THREE	"	Scammony Convolvulus.
FOUR	"	Smooth Crepis.
FIVE	"	Day Lily.
SIX	"	Hawkweed.
SEVEN	"	Small-cape Marigold.
EIGHT	"	Red Pimpernel.
NINE	"	Field Marigold.
TEN	"	Egyptian Fig Marigold.
ELEVEN	"	Star of Bethlehem.
NOON	....	Ice-plant.
ONE O'CLOCK	....	Profuse-flowering Pink.
TWO	"	Mouse-ear Hawkweed.
THREE	"	Dandelion.
FOUR	"	Madwort.
FIVE	"	Marvel of Peru.
SIX	"	Geranium.
SEVEN	"	Naked-stalked Poppy.
EIGHT	"	Upright Bindweed.
NINE	"	Flax-leaved Bindweed.
TEN	"	Cypress Vine.
ELEVEN	"	Night-flowering Catch-fly.

"I remember that I had considerable difficulty in learning this list. The same course was adopted with the days and months. Jacobus had told me that, in regard to the days, every one was at liberty to make his own calendar. I will give you ours. You can avail yourself of it," added she, directing, at the same time, a severe look towards the Pansy.

THE FLORAL WEEK.

MONDAY—Bladder Senna.
TUESDAY—Snowball.
WEDNESDAY—Barberry.
THURSDAY—Lilac.
FRIDAY—Cypress.
SATURDAY—Jonquille.
SUNDAY—Gilliflower.

"In regard to the months, the thing is perfectly simple. Nature herself has arranged this part of the calendar, by causing particular plants to bloom at certain seasons of the year.

THE CALENDAR OF FLORA.

JANUARY—Black Hellebore.
FEBRUARY—Mezereon.
MARCH—Alpine Soldanella.
APRIL—Early dwarf Tulip.
MAY—Common Dropwort.
JUNE—Cornpoppy.
JULY—Centaury.
AUGUST—Scabious.
SEPTEMBER—European Cyclamen.
OCTOBER—Chinese St. Johnswort.
NOVEMBER—Serrated Pallasia.
DECEMBER—Smooth Lopezia.

"Your father had returned from Paris, and my guardian was keeping me in close confinement. I was impatient, however, to know the issue of his journey. I bribed one of my keepers, and contrived to send the following letter to Jacobus:—

"'Full of socotrine aloe and touch-me-not, I must have, cost what it may, an Indian cane. My guardian assures me that you have given me over to the wind-flower. But I have hawthorn that this is a shameful bugloss. Ah! how much have I endured since our Virginian jessamine! Your presence will restore my buck-bean. No clematis shall again disturb our large broom-tape. I shall expect you in the ruins of the old castle, at yellow goats-beard precisely.'

"What I meant was this:—

"'I am full of grief and impatience. I must have an interview with you, cost what it may. My guardian assures me that you have deserted me. I hope that this is an infamous falsehood. How much have I suffered since we were separated! But your presence will restore my tranquility. No artifice shall hereafter disturb our union. I shall expect you in the ruins of the old castle, at precisely two o'clock.'

"I shall remember this all my life. It was a cypress of black hellebore,—or on a Friday in the month of January.

"I set out for the old ruined castle, and reached it just before yellow goats-beard, that is, before two had struck on the steeple-clock. I waited one hour—two hours—three hours,—but no one came. I called Jacobus, and echo alone answered my call. Seeing that night was at hand, I returned to my guardian, believing myself deserted, and resolved not to survive it. I accused your father of being unfaithful, Jacobus, when, in fact, the only one guilty was myself, or rather, the language of flowers.

"As I had not by me a poison sufficiently active, I put off my suicide till the morrow. Fortunate thought! The next day I was informed, that, at early dawn, the shepherds of the valley had found a man frozen, in the ruins of the old castle. This man was your father.

"Instead of writing to him,—'I shall expect you at mouse-ear hawkweed,' which means two o'clock in the afternoon, I had appointed the meeting at 'yellow goats-beard,' which means two o'clock in the morning.

"The flower-language had nearly caused the death of your father and your mother. You see to what the study of the languages may lead us. You see, too, how it was that your father bore all his life the mark of a frostbitten nose. And yet this did not prevent us from being happy, or from having a son."

Jacobus the son threw himself, weeping, into his mother's arms.

"And now, as I have shown you that I know more than she does," said the good dame, with a threatening look at the Pansy, "let me get my broom, that I may drive this poor wretch out of doors."

But the Pansy did not await the old woman's return. She had already departed in consternation, at having learned that her origin was merely the Paonosée.

Instead of representing the most exalted of human faculties, the poor flower was but the symbol of a vain and worthless beauty. It was enough to make one even less refined than the Pansy, disgusted with the world.

Jacobus had an attack of jaundice in consequence of the hoax which had thus been put upon him. He is yet in pursuit of that brilliant idea which is to make him cabinet-minister, or first valet de chambre to the king. France, which has so long been expecting an epic poem, must still rest satisfied with the Henriade.

The reader will find in the course of this work, the elements of that flower-language which is spoken at the present day by men of fancy, like Jacobus.

Alphabetical List of Flower Meanings

A.

English	French	Latin	Meaning
Windflower,	Anémone,	Anemone,	Abandonment.
Wormwood,	Absinthe,	Absinthium,	Absence.
Saffron,	Safran,	Crocus,	Abuse.
Thyme,	Thym,	Thymus,	Activity.
Daisy, double,	Paquerette double,	Bellis hortensis,	Affection.
Starwort,	Astère,	Aster,	Afterthought.
Sensitive Hedysarum,	Sainfoin oscillant,	Hedysarum gyranus,	Agitation.
Jessamine, common white,	Jasmin commun,	Jasminus officinale,	Amiability.
Anthericum,	Phalangère,	Phalangium,	Antidote.
Pimpernel, red,	Mouron rouge,	Anagallis phoenicea,	Appointment.
Arum,	Gouet, commun,	Arum vulgare,	Ardor.
Wake-robin,	Arum commun,	Arum commune,	Ardor.
Virgin's-bower,	Clématite,	Clematis,	Artifice.
Acanthus,	Acanthe,	Acanthus,	Arts.
Larch,	Mélèze,	Pinus Larix,	Audacity.
Meadow-saffron,	Colchique,	Colchicum,	Autumn.

Dodder,	Cuscute,	Cuscuta,	Baseness.
Sensitive plant,	Sensitive,	Mimosa sensitiva,	Bashfulness.
Rose,	Rose,	Rosa,	Beauty.
Passion-flower,	Grenadille bleue,	Passiflora cerulea,	Belief.
Cinquefoil,	Quinte-feuille,	Potentilla,	Beloved daughter.
Flax,	Lin,	Linum usitatissimum,	Benefactor.
Marshmallow,	Guimauve,	Althæa,	Beneficence.
Teasel,	Cardére,	Dipsacus fullonum,	Benefit.
Hyacinth, expanded,	Hyacinthe étalée,	Hyacinthus elatus,	Benevolence.
Manchineel,	Mancenillier,	Hippomanes mancinella,	Betrayal.
Dittany of Crete,	Dictame de Crete,	Origanum dictamnus,	Birth.
Aloes, socotrine,	Aloës, socotrine,	Aloe, succotrina,	Bitterness and pain.
Laburnum,	Cytise faux ébénier,	Cytisus laburnum,	Blackness.
Borage,	Bourrache,	Borago,	Bluntness.
Pine,	Pin,	Pinus,	Boldness.
Honeysuckle,	Chévre-feuille,	Lanicera caprifolium,	Bonds of love.

C.

English	French	Latin	Meaning
Madder,	Garance,	Rubia,	Calumny.
Violet, white,	Violette blanche,	Viola alba,	Candor.
Rose, musk,	Rose musquée,	Rosa moschata,	Capricious beauty.
Hortensia,	Hortensia,	Hortensia opuloides,	Carelessness.
Orange-blossom,	Fleur d'oranger,	Flos aurantii,	Chasity.
Pink, musk,	Œillet mignardise,	Dianthus moschatus,	Childishness.
Broom, Spanish,	Genêt d'Espagne,	Genista juncea,	Cleanliness.
Fig Marigold,	Ficoïde glaciale,	Mesembryanthemum chrystallinum,	Coldness of heart.
Chaste-tree,	Gattilier commun,	Vitex,	Coldness.
Motherwort,	Clandestine,	Lathræa clandestina,	Concealed love.
Lichen,	Hépatique,	Lichen hepatica,	Confidence.
Lime-tree,	Tilleul,	Tilia,	Conjugal affection.
Snowdrop,	Galanth perce-neige,	Galanthus nivalis,	Consolation.
Bellflower, pyramidal,	Pyramidale bleue,	Campanula pyramidalis,	Constancy.
Day-lily, yellow,	Belle de jour,	Hemerocallis flava,	Coquetry.
Poplar, black,	Peuplier noir,	Populus niger,	Courage.
Elastic Momordica,	Momordique élastique,	Momordica elaterium,	Critique; hoax.
Nettle,	Ortie,	Urtica,	Cruelty.
Tiger-flower,	Tigridie,	Tigridia,	Cruelty.
Balsam of Peru,	Baume du Perou,	Myroxylon,	Cure.

D.

English	French	Latin	Meaning
Strawberry of the Indies,	Fraise de l'Inde,	Fragaria indica,	Deceitful appearances.
Thornapple,	Datura,	Datura stramonium,	Deceitful charms.
Daffodil, common,	Narcisse des près,	Narcissus sylvestris,	Deceitful hopes.
Tulip,	Tulipe,	Tulipia,	Declaration of love.
Hogbean,	Jusquiame,	Hyoscyamus,	Defect.
Bluebottle,	Bluet,	Centaurea cyanus,	Delicacy.
Laurestine,	Lauier-tin,	Viburnum tinus,	Delicate attentions.
Hybrid crinum,	Crinole hybride,	Crinum,	Delicate weakness.
Mezereon,	Lauréole bois gentil,	Daphne mezereum,	Desire to please.
Jonquille,	Jonquille,	Narcissus jonquilla,	Desire.
Mulberry, black,	Muier noir,	Morus niger,	Devotedness.
Ophrys, spider,	Ophrise-arraignée,	Ophrys arachnites,	Dexterity.
Black thorn,	Epine noire,	Prunus sylvestris,	Difficulty.
Clove-tree,	Giroflier,	Caryophyllus aromaticus,	Dignity.
Maidenhair,	Capillaire,	Adiantum,	Discretion.
Lavender,	Lavande aspic,	Lavandula spica,	Distrust.
Rosebay,	Laurier-rose,	Nerium oleander,	Distrust.
Virginian Cowslip,	Gyroselle,	Dodocatheon meadia,	Divinity.
Fieldrush,	Jonc des champs,	Juncus campestris,	Docility.
Poppy, white,	Pavot blanc,	Papaver albus,	Dormant affection.
Daisy, wild,	Marguerite des près,	Bellis perennis,	Dost thou love me?
Dragon-plant,	Arum serpentaire,	Arum dracunculus,	Dread.
Cornel-tree,	Cornouiller,	Cornus,	Duration.

Lilac,	Lilas commun,	Lilac vulgaris,	Earliest love.
Primrose,	Primevère,	Primula,	Early youth.
Cherry-tree,	Cerisier,	Cerasus,	Education.
Acacia, rose,	Acacia, rose,	Acacia, rosea,	Elegance.
Water-lily, white,	Nénuphar blanc,	Nymphæa alba,	Eloquence.
Ipomea, scarlet,	Ipomée écarlate,	Ipomæa coccinea,	Embrace.
Bindweed, purple,	Liseron pourpre,	Convolvulus purpureus,	Eminence.
Gilliflower, stock,	Giroflée des jardins,	Cheiranthus incanus,	Enduring beauty.
Snowball,	Boule de neige,	Viburnum opulus,	Ennui.
Bramble,	Ronce,	Rubus,	Envy.
Poppy, corn,	Pavot coquelicot,	Papaver rhæas,	Ephemeral charms.
Sage,	Sauge,	Salvia,	Esteem.

F.

English	French	Latin	Meaning
Valerian, red,	Valériane rouge,	Valerian rubra,	Facility.
Wall-flower,	Giroflée jaune,	Cheiranthus cheiri,	Faithful in misfortune.
Sunflower,	Soleil, [Tournesol]*	Helianthus,	False riches.
Bugloss,	Buglosse,	Anchusa,	Falsehood.
Parsley,	Persil,	Apium,	Feast.
Sweet Sultan, yellow,	Centaurée-amberboi,	Centaurea moschata,	Felicity.
Speedwell,	Véronique élégante,	Veronica amœna,	Fidelity.
Dittany, white,	Fraxinelle,	Dictamnus,	Fire.
Iris, flaming,	Iris flambe,	Iris flammea,	Flame.
Venus's Looking-glass,	Miroir de Venus,	Campanula speculum,	Flattery.
Columbine,	Ancolie,	Aquilegia,	Folly.
Zephyranth,	Zéphyranthe,	Zephyranthes,	Fond Caresses.
Pomegranate,	Grenadier,	Punica granatum,	Foppery.
Holly,	Houx,	Ilex,	Forecast.
Honesty,	Lunaire,	Lunaria,	Forgetfulness.
Ladies' Ear-drop,	Fuchsia,	Fuchsia,	Frailty.
Syringa,	Syringa,	Philadelphus,	Fraternal regard.
Ivy,	Lierre,	Hedera helix,	Friendship.
Grass, quaking,	Brise tremblante,	Briza media,	Frivolity.
Bladder-senna,	Baguenaudier,	Colutea arborescens,	Frivolous amusement.
Enchanter's Nightshade,	Circée,	Cichorium intybus,	Frugality.
Succory,	Chicorée-amére,	Cichorium intybus,	Frugality.
Hollyhock,	Rose trémière,	Alcea rosea,	Fruitfulness.

*The correct name is Tournesol. Soleil means sun. [Ed.]

Funitory,	Fumeterre commune,	Fumaria,
Nosegay,	Bouquet,	Florum fasciculus,
Orange-tree,	Oranger,	Aurantium,
Plane-tree,	Platane,	Platanus,
Rose, Provence,	Rose pompon,	Rosa provincialis,
Laurel,	Laurier franc,	Laurus,
Strawberry,	Fraise,	Fragaria,
Rose, hundred-leaved,	Rose cent-feuille,	Rosa centifolia,
Japan rose,	Camellia,	Camellia japonica,
Ash,	Frêne èlevè,	Fraxinus excelsior,
Aspen,	Peuplier tremble,	Populus tremula,
Water-lily, yellow,	Nymphea jaune,	Nymphæa lutea,

G.

Gall.
Gallantry.
Generosity.
Genius.
Gentillessee.
Glory.
Goodness.
Graces.
Gratitude.
Greatness.
Groan.
Growing indifference.

H.

Mugwort,	Armoise,	Artemisia,	Happiness.
Wild-service,	Alisier,	Cratægus torminalis,	Harmony.
Thistle,	Chardon,	Carduus,	Harshness.
Basil,	Basilic,	Ocimum,	Hatred.
Rosemary,	Romarin,	Rosmarinus,	Healing balm.
Fir,	Sapin,	Abies,	Height.
Milkwort,	Polygala,	Polygala,	Hermitage.
Coriander,	Coriandre,	Coriandrum,	Hidden worth.
Hawthorn,	Aubêpine,	Cratægus oxyacantha,	Hope.
Oak,	Chêne,	Quercus,	Hospitality.
Bindweed, field,	Liseron des champs,	Convolvulus arvensis,	Humility.

I.

Prickly-pear,	Raquette-figuier d'Inde,	Cactus opuntia,	I burn.
Star of Bethlehem,	Ornithogale,	Ornithogalum,	Idleness.
Amaranth,	Amaranthe,	Amaranthus,	Immortality.
Celsia, great flowered,	Celsie à Crete,	Celsia cretica,	Immortality.
Touch-me-not,	Balsamine,	Impatiens,	Impatience.
Burdock,	Bardane,	Arctium Lappa,	Importunity.
Reed,	Roseau,	Arundo,	Imprudence; music.
Tree Primrose,	Onagre,	Œnothera,	Inconstancy.
Prune, wild,	Prunier sauvage,	Prunus sylvestris,	Independence.
Persian Candy-tuft,	Ibéride de Perse,	Iberis semperflorens,	Indifference.
Bellflower,	Campanule,	Campanula,	Indiscretion.
Rose, yellow,	Rose jaune,	Rosa lutea,	Infidelity.
Crowfoot, marsh,	Renoncule scélérate,	Ranunculus sceleratus,	Ingratitude.
Hop,	Houblon,	Humulus lupulus,	Injustice.
Daisy, single,	Paquerette simple,	Bellis simplex,	Innocence.
Angelica,	Angelique,	Angelica,	Inspiration.
Goosefoot,	Anserine ambroisée,	Chenopodium,	Insult.
Grape-vine,	Vigne,	Vitis,	Intoxication.

J.

Balm,	Melisse citronelle,	Melissa officinalis,	Joke.
Wood-sorrel,	Oxalide-alléluia,	Oxalis acetocella,	Joy.
Chestnut-tree,	Chataignier,	Castanea,	Justice.
Coltsfoot, sweet-scented,	Tussilage odorant,	Tussilago fragrans,	Justice.

K.

Violet Ivy,	Cobée grimpante,	Coboea scandens,	Knots.

L.

Larkspur,	Pied d'alouette,	Delphinium,	Levity.
Lucerne,	Luzerne,	Medicago,	Life.
Spindle-tree,	Fusain,	Evonymus vulgaris,	Likeness.
Tulip, virgin,	Tulipe vierge,		Literary debut.
Myrtle,	Myrte,	Myrtus,	Love.
Chestnut-tree, horse,	Marronnier d'Inde,	Æsculus hippocastanum,	Luxury.

M.

English	French	Latin	Meaning
lily,	Lis,	Lilium,	Majesty.
Rue,	Rue Sauvage,	Ruta graveolens,	Manners.
Cactus,	Cactier,	Cactus,	Maternal love.
Geranium,clouded,	Géranium triste,	Geranium nubilum,	Melancholy.
Iris,	Iris,	Iris,	Message.
Broom, prickly,	Genêt épineux,	Genista spiniflora,	Misanthropy.
Ophrys, fly,	Ophrise-mouche,	Ophrys myoides,	Mistake.
Woad,	Réséda,	Reseda,	Modest merit.
Violet, sweet,	Violette odorante,	Viola odorata,	Modesty.
Cypress,	Cyprès,	Cupressus,	Mourning.

N.

English	French	Latin	Meaning
Catch-fly, night-flowering,	Siléné, fleur de nuit,	Silene nocturna,	Night.
Dahlia,	Dahlia,	Dahlia,	Novelty.

O.

English	French	Latin	Meaning
Rest-harrow,	Bugrane arrête-bœuf,	Ononis,	Obstacle.
Foxglove,	Digitale,	Digitalis,	Occupation.
Dandelion,	Pissenlit,	Leontodon,	Oracle.
Hornbeam,	Charme,	Carpinus,	Ornament.

Southernwood,	Citronelle,	Artemisia abrotanum,	Pain.
Pheasant's-eye,	Adonide,	Adonis,	Painful remembrance.
Mistletoe,	Gui,	Viscum album,	Parasite.
Dock,	Patience,	Rumex,	Patience.
Olive,	Olivier,	Oliva,	Peace.
Pineapple,	Ananas,	Bromelia ananas,	Perfection.
Bird cherry-tree,	Lauier-amandier,	Prunus padus,	Perfidy.
Crowfoot, meadow,	Renoncule, bouton d'or,	Ranunculus aeris,	Perfidy.
Everlasting,	Gnaphale,	Gnaphalium,	Perpetual remembrances.
Acacia,	Acacia,	Acacia,	Platonic love.
Hyacinth, wild,	Hyacinthe sauvage,	Hyacinthus sylvestris,	Play.
Wild Rose-tree,	Eglantier,		Poetical person.
Rose, wild,	Eglantine,	Rosa canina,	Poetry.
Crown-imperial,	Couronne impériale,	Fritillaria imperialis,	Power.
Geranium, rose,	Géranium rose,	Geranium roseum,	Preference.
Marigold, cape,	Souci pluvial,	Calendula pluvialis,	Presage.
Toad-flax,	Muflier,	Antirrhinum,	Presumption.
Willow-herb, purple,	Salicaire,	Lythrum salicaria,	Pretension.
Lily, daffodil,	Amaryllis jaune,	Amaryllis lutea,	Pride.
Jamaica Plum,	Myrobalan,	Spondias myrobalanus,	Privation.
Rosebay, Willow-herb,	Epilobe à épi,	Epilobium spicatum,	Production.
Privet,	Troëne,	Ligustrum,	Prohibition.

62

English	French	Latin	Meaning
			P. cont'd
Prune-tree,	Prunier,	Prunus,	Promise.
Gilliflower, Mahon,	Giroflée de Mahon,	Cheiranthus mahoneus,	Promptness.
Beech-tree,	Hêtre commun,	Fagus sylvatica,	Prosperity.
Mulberry, white,	Murier blanc,	Morus albus,	Prudence.
Star of Bethlehem, pyramidal,	Ornithogale pyramidale,	Ornithogalum pyramidale,	Purity.
			Q.
Buck-bean,	Menyanthe,	Menyanthes,	Quiet; repose.
			R.
Goats-rue,	Galéga,	Galega,	Reason.
Hazel,	Noisettier,	Corylus,	Reconciliation.
King's-spear,	Asphodèle jaune,	Asphodelus,	Regret.
Indian cane,	Balisier,	Arundo bambos,	Rendezvous.
Maple,	Erable champêtre,	Acer,	Reserve.
Date-plum,	Plaqueminier,	Diospyros,	Resistance.
Lily of the Valley,	Muguet de Mai,	Convallaria maialis,	Return of happiness.
Osmunda,	Osmonde,	Osmunda,	Revery.
Wreath of Roses,	Couronne de roses,	Corona rosarum,	Reward of virtue.
Wheat,	Blé,	Triticum,	Riches.
Ladies' Bedstraw,	Grateron,	Galium,	Rudeness.
Polemonium,	Polémoine bleue,	Polemonium ceruleum,	Rupture.

S.

Weeping-willow,	Saule pleureur,	Sadness.
Yew,	If,	Sadness.
Mandrake,	Mandragore,	Scarcity.
Sweet William,	Œillet de poéte,	Scorn.
Hair-moss,	Polytric á urne,	Secret.
American Aloe,	Agavé,	Security.
Narcissus, white,	Narcisse des poétes,	Selfishness.
Jessamine, Spanish,	Jasmin d'Espagne,	Sensuality.
Ash-leaved Trumpet-flower,	Jasmin de Virginie,	Separation.
Viburnum, prickly,	Camara piquant,	Severity.
Peony, common,	Pivoine officinale,	Shame.
Wood Anemone,	Anémone des prés,	Sickness.
Rose, white,	Rose blanche	Silence.
Rose, single,	Rose simple,	Simplicity.
Silver-weed,	Argentine,	Simplicity.
Fern,	Fougère,	Sincerity.
Aloes, parrot-bill,	Aloès, bee de perroquet,	Small talk.
Arum, fly-catching,	Arum, gobe-mouche,	Snare.

Salix babylonica,	
Taxus,	
Atropa mandragora,	
Dianthus barbatus,	
Polytrichum,	
Agave Americana,	
Narcissus poeticus,	
Jasminum grandiflorum,	
Bignonia radicans,	
Lantana aculeata,	
Pæonia officinalis,	
Anemone nemorosa,	
Rosa alba,	
Rosa berberifolia,	
Potentilla anserina,	
Filix,	
Arum crinitum,	

S. cont'd

Heath,	Bruyére commune,	Erica vulgaris,	Solitude.
Vervain,	Verveine,	Verbena,	Sorcery.
Barberry,	Epine-vinette,	Berberis,	Sourness.
Rose capucine,	Rose capucine,		Splendor.
Box,	Buis,	Buxus,	Stoicism.
Fennel,	Fenouil,	Anethum fœniculum,	Strength.
Geranium, scarlet,	Géranium écarlate,	Geranium coccineum,	Stupidity.
Juniper,	Genévrier,	Juniperus,	Succor.
Bryony,	Tame commun,	Tamus communis,	Support.
Round-leaved Sundew,	Rossolis à feuilles rondes,	Drosera rotundifolia,	Surprise.
Thornapple, purple,	Stramoine fastueuse,	Datura fastuosa,	Suspicion.
Periwinkle,	Pervenche,	Vinca,	Sweet remembrance.
Sea-lavender,	Staticé maritim,	Statice limonium,	Sympathy.

Helenium, smooth,	Hélénie d'automne,	Helenium autumnale,	Tears.
Currant,	Groseiller,	Ribes rubrum,	Thankfulness.
Turnsol,	Héliotrope,	Heliotropium,	The intoxication of love.
Hyacinth, garden,	Hyacinthe d'Orient,	Hyacinthus orientalis,	The language of flowers.
Pansy,	Pensée,	Viola tricolor,	Thought.
Almond-tree,	Amandier,	Amygdalus,	Thoughtlessness.
Poplar, white,	Peuplier blanc,	Populus alba,	Time.
Marvel of Peru,	Belle de nuit,	Mirabilis,	Timidity.
Madder, yellow,	Alysse saxatile,	Alyssum saxatile,	Tranquility.
Virginian Spiderwort,	Ephémérine de Virginie,	Tradescantia Virginica,	Transient felicity.
Whortleberry,	Airelle myrtille,	Vaccinium,	Treachery.
Marigold, garden,	Souci commun,	Calendula officinalis,	Trouble.
Pink, clove,	Œillet des fleuristes,	Dianthus caryophyllus,	True love.
Hepatica,	Anemone hépatique,	Anemone hepatica,	Trust.
Nightshade,	Morelle,	Solanum,	Truth.

U.

Rose, perpetual,	Rose des quatre saisons,	Rosa perpetua,	Unfading beauty.
Immortal flowers,	Immortelle,	Xeranthemum annuum,	Unfading remembrance.
Broom-rape,	Orobanche majeure,	Orobanche major,	Union.
Pink, yellowish,	Œillet jaune,	Dianthus luteus,	Unreasonableness.
Meadow-sweet,	Spirée ulmaire,	Spiræa ulmaria,	Uselessness.
Grass,	Gazon,	Gramen,	Utility.

V.

Aster, china,	Marguerite-reine,	Aster chinensis,	Variety.
Tares,	Ivraie,	Vicia,	Vice.
Rose, moss,	Rose mosseuse,	Rosa muscosa,	Voluptuous love.
Tuberose,	Tubéreuse,	Polyanthes,	Voluptuousness.

W.

Milfoil,	Achillée,	Achillea,	War.
Peppermint,	Menthe poivrée,	Mentha piperita,	Warmth of feeling.
Rose, striped,	Rose panachée,	Rosa variegata,	Warmth of heart.
Hollowroot,	Adoxa,	Adoxa moschatellina,	Weakness.
Water-lily, peltated,	Nélumbo,	Nymphæa nelumbo,	Wisdom.
Christmas aconite,	Hellebore de Noël,	Helleborus,	Wit.
Pasque-flower,	Coquelourde,	Anemone pulsatilla,	Without pretension.

Y.

Rosebud,	Bouton de rose,	Rosæ calyx,	Young girl.
Lilac, white,	Lilas blanc,	Lilac alba,	Youth.

The Pansy

meaning: *Thought*

hand-colored illustration
engraved on steel by J.N. Gimbrede
from designs by J.J. Grandville for *Les Fleurs Animees*

introduction by Alphonse Kerr
text by Taxile Delord
translated by N. Cleaveland
published by M. Martin in New York as
The Flowers Personified—1847

visit www.earthlypursuits.com
for more of *The Flowers Personified*

www.ingramcontent.com/pod-product-compliance
Lightning Source LLC
Chambersburg PA
CBHW071223170626
46809CB00005BA/1918